Gwendolyn's Gifts

By Patty Sheehan

Illustrated by
Claudia Bumgarner-Kirby

PELICAN PUBLISHING COMPANY
Gretna 1991

Pelican edition, 1991

Library of Congress Cataloging-in-Publication Data

Sheehan, Patty, 1945-
    Gwendolyn's gifts / by Patty Sheehan; illustrated by
Claudia Bumgarner-Kirby.
        p. cm.
    Summary: Bored with her royal role, Queen Gwendolyn finds
fulfillment through developing and combining her own abilities
into a creative and nontraditional lifestyle.
    ISBN 0-88289-845-0
    [1. Kings, queens, rulers, etc.—Fiction. 2. Artists—
Fiction.]
I. Bumgarner-Kirby, Claudia, ill. II. Title.
PZ7.S5395Gw 1991
[E]—dc20   91-12335
                                                      CIP
                                                       AC

First printing 1988 by Program for Assistance in Equity, a
joint project of the University of New Mexico and the New
Mexico State Department of Education, Vocational-Technical
and Adult Education.

Manufactured in Hong Kong

Published by Pelican Publishing Company, Inc.
1101 Monroe Street, Gretna, Louisiana 70053

To the creative child in everyone, and to the children from the Albuquerque public schools who inspired this story.

GWENDOLYN'S GIFTS

"Elegant, simply elegant," exclaimed King Cornelius, admiring the poached eggs. "Not too hard and not too soft. And these raspberry preserves are delectable!"

Queen Gwendolyn slouched back in her throne and sighed, "I'm bored!"

"Perhaps you need a change, my dear," replied King Cornelius. "I'll order the castle seamstress to make you a new gown to wear at once."

The next day Queen Gwendolyn went to the sewing room to see how the new gown was coming along. The seamstress was humming merrily as she cut and stitched.

Queen Gwendolyn was intrigued with every bit of delicate lace and ribbon and each shiny button. She imagined trimming the gown herself. She would make flowers of lace, and birds of ribbons and buttons. "May I help?" she asked eagerly.

"Oh no, your majesty," replied the woman. "Tis but the work of a lowly seamstress, certainly not fit for a queen!"

So Queen Gwendolyn just watched. But she watched every move the seamstress made, until the most elegant gown she had ever seen was finished.

She wore her new gown all the next morning and all the next afternoon, while King Cornelius decided which of the royal chef's new recipes still needed improvement.

That evening, Queen Gwendolyn said to King Cornelius, "I'm bored!"

"Perhaps you need a change, my dear," replied King Cornelius. "I'll order the crown jeweler to make you a new crown at once."

The next day, Queen Gwendolyn went down to the castle jeweler's shop to see how the new crown was coming along. She watched the jeweler concentrating silently as he carefully examined and polished the rubies, diamonds, and emeralds.

Queen Gwendolyn longed to hold each jewel and place it into the golden crown. "May I help?" she asked eagerly.

"Oh no, your majesty," replied the man. "'Tis but the work of a lowly jeweler, certainly not fit for a queen!"

So Queen Gwendolyn just watched. But she watched every move the jeweler made, until the most elegant crown she had ever seen was finished.

She wore her new crown all the next morning and all the next afternoon, while King Cornelius awaited the royal chef's third attempt to create the perfect cherry-cream torte.

That evening, Queen Gwendolyn said to King Cornelius, "I'm bored!"

"Perhaps you need a change, my dear," replied King Cornelius. "I'll order the castle carpenter to make you a new throne at once."

The next day, Queen Gwendolyn went down to the castle carpentry shop to see how the new throne was coming along. She watched the carpenter saw and hammer and nail. She listened to him whistling happily as he began to carve beautiful designs into the wood.

Queen Gwendolyn wanted to carve a dragon into the back of the throne with the carpenter's knife. "May I help?" she asked eagerly.

"Oh no, your majesty," replied the man. "'Tis but the work of a lowly carpenter, certainly not fit for a queen!"

So Queen Gwendolyn just watched. But she watched every move the carpenter made, until the most elegant throne she had ever seen was finished.

She sat on her new throne all the next morning and all the next afternoon, and that evening she said to King Cornelius, "I'm still bored!"

"Perhaps you need a change, my dear," replied King Cornelius. "I'll order a carriage to take you to the city. You can visit your cousin, the duchess, for a few days."

Queen Gwendolyn thought for a moment, and with a twinkle in her eye, she said, "Good idea. I would love to go on a vacation."

Late the next morning, as the carriage drove through the country, Queen Gwendolyn ordered the driver to stop at a farmhouse. "I'll stay here tonight," she told him. "Please come back for me in the morning."

Inside the farmhouse, the queen said to the farmer's wife, "If you will give me a room for the night, some cloth, and a needle and thread, I will give you my elegant new crown."

The farmer's wife seemed delighted to have a crown of her own, and did as Queen Gwendolyn requested.

All afternoon and on into the night the queen sat and sewed. Now *she* was humming merrily as she made herself a simple peasant's dress to wear.

As instructed, the driver arrived the next morning, and Queen Gwendolyn, very pleased with her new clothes, got into the carriage. Just before they reached the city, she said, "Stop at the city jeweler's shop, and come back for me at sunset."

There, Queen Gwendolyn, disguised as a peasant, asked the jeweler if she could work for a day. She learned all she could about the glistening jewels and precious metals. She worked, concentrating silently, just as the jeweler did. And, at the end of the day, the jeweler paid her three silver coins.

When the driver arrived, he asked, "Now shall I take you to the duchess's home?"

But Queen Gwendolyn, who had no intention of visiting the duchess, said, "No, take me to the inn. I shall sleep there. Please return for me tomorrow morning at sunrise."

The next morning, Queen Gwendolyn proudly paid the innkeeper the three silver coins she had earned. "Take me to the city carpenter's shop," she told the driver. "Come back for me at sunset. Then we shall return to the castle."

At the carpentry shop, Queen Gwendolyn, again disguised as a peasant, asked to work for a day. Whistling happily, she sawed, hammered, and nailed the wood and even carved herself a beautiful sign.

At sunset, the driver returned. They drove past the city jeweler's shop, the inn, and the farmer's house.

When King Cornelius came out to greet them at the castle, he was most surprised to see…

Queen Gwendolyn in the driver's seat!

Queen Gwendolyn told King Cornelius all about her vacation. Then she pounded her sign into the ground and said, "You were right. I did need a change. I'm going to open my own shop. It will be called 'Gwendolyn's Gifts.' I'll make all the gifts myself!"

Nowadays, things are different at the castle. People come from far and near to buy the lovely gifts that Queen Gwendolyn makes from cloth and wood and precious metals and jewels.

Sometimes Queen Gwendolyn gets so busy in her shop that she forgets to stop for dinner until...

Delicious aromas remind her that King Cornelius, who has now become a gourmet cook, is bringing her an elegant tray!